T0070214

GOD!
WHERE WERE YOU?

PATRICIA BASKERVILLE

authorHOUSE®

AuthorHouse™
1663 Liberty Drive
Bloomington, IN 47403
www.authorhouse.com
Phone: 1 (800) 839-8640

Published by AuthorHouse 08/23/2017

ISBN: 978-1-5462-0501-2 (sc)
ISBN: 978-1-5462-0500-5 (e)

Library of Congress Control Number: 2017912902

Print information available on the last page.

Any people depicted in stock imagery provided by Thinkstock are models, and such images are being used for illustrative purposes only. Certain stock imagery © Thinkstock.

This book is printed on acid-free paper.

Scriptures used are taken from the King James Version of the Bible.

CONTENTS

# DEDICATION

This book is dedicated to my son Darius Allen Baskerville, who encouraged me to complete this book. I also dedicate this book to my mother Pastor Maybelle Salters, who has instilled inside of me that "I can do all things through Christ which strengtheneth me" Philippians 4:13."

INTRODUCTION

We live in a world where life at times seems so cruel and unfair. It is as if doing and saying all the right things does not seem to count for very much. At times, it seems as if no matter what you do, you always end up with the short end of the stick; resulting in finding yourself in a no win situation. I have been taught from a small child to trust in God, and he will take care of any situation that seems too hard to bear. However, there are times when we experience personal tragedies, which challenge our faith as to the very existence of God. During those difficult periods within our lives, we tend to say, "If God is so real and loving, why did he allow this to happen?" We begin to blame God for our tragic situation and circumstances. A man named Job in the Bible experienced extreme tragic circumstances, which should have caused him to question the existence of God.

It seemed so unfair that a man who loved God and walked upright before him should lose everything and everyone he loved. In one instance, he went from a wealthy man with children to a man who has lost all his wealth and children. The only family member that remained in his life was his wife. Unlike most spouses who have experienced a loss of some kind, Job's wife was not sympathetic, compassionate, or encouraging. People that exhibit the behavior that Job's wife illustrated tends to be negative in their speech and views. In their tongue lies venom, which speaks death and doom to a situation and not life. They are detrimental to one's emotional state. Also, people of such immoral character will encourage negative attitude and speech to curse or blame God for tragic circumstances. It seemed as if God had left Job to the wiles of Satan.

It looked like life had dealt Job a dirty hand and God had left him hanging. However, that was not true. God was there all the time. He was bragging on his vessel of honor Job. Many of us have experienced such times in our lives whereas; everyone closest to us seems to have abandoned us, including God. What we fail to realize is that when all hell is breaking loose in our lives, that is when **God is bragging on us!** He has a master plan for us that is far greater than we can ever imagine. Therefore, he allows the devil to test us in ways that we could not begin to imagine. God knows what he has instilled inside of us and knows that we could pass the test with excellence. Growing up with a preacher for a mom, I was taught that God is everywhere. I remember the older mothers in the church saying that, "God will never leave you nor forsake you." I also remember them saying that "God is seldom early, he is never late, but he is always on time."

As Christians, we know this to be true in our hearts. However, when we are waiting on God to resolve something or answer us, it seems like he takes forever to respond. We go to the church seeking encouragement and strength by assembling ourselves with our sisters and brothers in Christ. Sometimes instead we find nasty, mean, hateful and spiteful Christians. You begin to wonder how can people who say they love God, called by God, anointed, and appointed by God act so ugly in God's house. Seemingly the numbers of cantankerous Christians outnumber the kind and loving Christians within the body of Christ. It will make you wonder if you are spiritually retarded and everyone is spiritually correct? With a sorrowful heart, you begin to ask this question "GOD! WHERE ARE YOU?"

Reader, if you have found yourself experiencing any of the above situations, I pray that the words written in this book will serve as a source of encouragement and inspiration. No matter what you may be going through, keep in mind that God is closer to you than the breath in your body; even when it seems he is so far away. I am a personal witness of this.

God Bless You!

The author

CHAPTER 1

The Jungle

Anita grew up in the rural part of the city. She was the oldest of five children, four girls, and one boy. Her mother was a homemaker, and Anita's father was a mechanic. They lived in a low-income housing development. Anita was thirteen years old and in her second year of middle school when her life seemed to have turned upside down. Anita was a very attractive young lady; however, she was a tomboy at heart. She was always climbing trees, racing her bike, and wrestling with the boys. Anita was petite, but she was very strong physically. The boys she wrestled with were not able to subdue her in any way. Anita however, was not aware of the fact that a local female gang leader was watching her. One morning during homeroom the gang leader along with some other gang members had entered one of Anita's classrooms illegally. The gang proceeded towards where Anita sat in the classroom. The female gang leader introduces herself to Anita. She had complimented Anita on her fighting abilities. The female gang leader offered

Anita the opportunity to join them. Anita had refused the female gang leader's offer to join the gang.

The offer to join the gang was recanted, and a threat was issued instead by the female gang leader. The female gang leader told Anita she would either join them or fight one of them every day for the rest of her life. The female gang leader stressed to Anita that no one refused the gang. The female gang leader told Anita that if she fought one of them and won, the next time Anita would have to fight more than one gang member. Each time Anita won a fight against any number of gang members, the numbers would increase until she joined them or they kill her. Anita joined the gang after the issued threat. Her nightmare was just beginning. Anita went home from school that day with fear in her heart. As she entered the small five-room apartment, she found her mother on her knees praying; this was not uncommon. Anita's mother could be found every day at the same time on her knees praying for the safe return of her children from school. Her mother was a prayer warrior and an associated minister in her local church. After the last child arrived home safely, Anita's mother would rise from off her knees, and give God thanks for bringing her children safely home.

Anita's mom would ask how their day went and proceeded to help them with their homework. Her mom would then serve dinner. Dinner was always prepared by the time the children arrived home from school. Anita's family did not have much money, but they never went without food and clothing. There was a hot meal served each morning for breakfast, during lunch, and at dinner time. Her father did not believe in eating out. Therefore, her mother cooked every meal seven days a week. Anita wanted to share what had happened to her with her mother, but she was afraid that some of the gang members might come after one of her siblings. Therefore, Anita decided to keep the events of her day to herself. As the days went on Anita witnessed many stabbings, shootings, and blood baths that resulted from gang rivalry. Anita never stabbed or shot anyone, but she did participate in physical gang fights involving chains, knives, and pipes. God was with Anita. She always came out of a fight with no more than a minor scratch. Whenever the police showed up, she always managed to get away.

Anita had a praying mom. She could hear her mother praying aloud in the bathroom early in the morning before anyone got up. Her prayer was, "Lord protect my children today from all harm and danger, seen and unseen, and Lord, please hold back the hands of death from my children." That prayer spared Anita's life many days. Anita was getting comfortable being in the gang. She liked the power and prestige that came with gang association. The gang members wore denim jackets with the gang's insignia on attached. Other students knew who the gang members were and they avoided them. Anita wore her gang jacket on school property only, in between classes and after school. She made an agreement with another gang member to keep her jacket at the gang member's home. Anita knew that if her parents saw that jacket, they would realize that she was in a gang. Anita knew that the consequences would result in corporal punishment. Anita also knew that she would be forced to leave the gang regardless of the circumstances. Anita was a child who never fit in anywhere. She always wanted to be a part of something and have a feeling of belonging. Unfortunately, she felt a part of something that was dangerous and deadly. Becoming a member of a gang was one of the biggest mistakes of Anita's life. Anita's joining a gang lead to heavier things, trying to prove that she was a team player of the gang. Anita began smoking cigarettes because it was what the gang members did. Some gang members that were taking a draw from a marijuana cigarette persuaded Anita to try some. She took part in this ritual twice. The second time she took a draw from a marijuana joint her head began to feel funny.

Anita made a promise to God that if he would allow her to overcome the strangeness, she experienced because of smoking the second joint, that she would never do it again. Anita suspected the marijuana joint was laced with something. Anita came close to getting raped several times. She would dance seductively, grinding her body against male gang members. When the young men reacted to her advances and wanted to go further, Anita would back away. Her actions were dangerous, considering the age of the males she was dancing with seductively. Anita was only thirteen, and many of the male gang members were at least four to five years older than she was and the young men were sexually active. She was a good tease and was not willing to sleep with any of the males. Anita was adamant about waiting until she got married to have sex. Anita's parents were very strict;

however, she found time to engage in mischief on days she had cheerleading practice. There were times she would go to practice but never remained for the entire session. Anita was her teachers' pet including the captain of the cheerleading squad, which made it convenient for her to leave early without being penalized. Anita's parents had no idea of what she was doing behind their backs. She did not fit the bill of a child who was involved in the things that she did behind their backs. Anita was a straight A student and made the honor roll every month in school. Anita never had any friends calling the house. Her parents never allowed any of their children to spend the night out at anyone's house.

Despite a strict household, Anita found ways to consort with gang members. Her mother took them to church every Sunday and Bible study every Thursday night. Anita's mother joined a local Pentecostal church when Anita was five years old. It was an old fashion holiness church, where they spoke in tongues, prophesied, and danced in the spirit. They were not allowed to wear pants, makeup, open toe shoes, and jewelry, not even a wedding band. Anita's mother was an associate minister and the church prophetess. God showed her mother explicit things concerning peoples' lives. Anita sat in church with great fear hoping and praying that God would not reveal to her mother the things she was doing. Anita had encountered another problem far worse than being a gang member. She, unfortunately, had the displeasure of her pastor coming on to her sexually. Anita's pastor asked her mother, one Sunday after morning fellowship if he could have a word with Anita in his study privately. Her mother trusted the pastor and therefore gave permission for her daughter to go and speak with him privately. Anita was surprised and very uncomfortable concerning the conversation her pastor was having with her.

The pastor began to compliment her on how pretty she had looked and was looking her up and down. He continued to compliment her on how she was physically filling out anatomically. The pastor then proceeded to ask her had she ever had sex before. Anita was crushed, horrified, and shocked at what came out of his mouth. She had always looked up to her pastor as being a great man of God. The pastor told her that God had given him a special prophetic word to give her. He told Anita that God told him that he had to be the first male to open her womb. The pastor began to speak in tongues and repeatedly said to her, that God said I must be the first to have sex with you. He then laid hands on her and began to pray for her. While praying the pastor said to Anita that, God said she was not to tell anyone about his conversation with her. The pastor told Anita that if she were to tell anyone that God would give him the power to send an Angel to her home and kill her entire family. The pastor began speaking in tongues again. Anita did not know the Bible that well. Therefore she believed him. She thought he could send an Angel out to kill the family. After all, Anita saw him pray for people, and they got healed; prophesied to people and the prophecy happened. The pastor appeared to be a great man of God to Anita, and she was afraid of him.

However, she was confused about the sex part. Anita's mother always taught her that sex before or outside of marriage was wrong. Anita was confused and scared and could not tell anyone. Anita hoped and prayed that God would reveal the conversation that occurred in the pastor's office to her mother. Anita thought of telling some of her gang members and having the pastor killed. However, Anita feared that God would kill her if she had one of his preachers killed. The pastor had twelve children with his wife, who was his high school sweetheart. Seven of his children were grown up and married. Five of them were living at home. Only his set of twins were younger than Anita. The Pastor at that time was a sixty-two-year-old man, who jogged every morning for an hour. He worked out at the gym twice a week. The pastor was physically fit for his age. This pastor began to make his move on Anita. The pastor would take all the children in the church to the movies once a month. He would sit a few rows behind the children, supposedly chaperoning them. While in the movie theater the pastor would request that Anita sat next to him. His excuse was that her parents were overly protective of her and he had to keep a close eye on her. Anita out of fear went and sat next to him. The pastor would hold her hands massaging them up and down as he held them. He then began rubbing her thigh in the dark movie theater. There were times when he rubbed her thigh, and his hands almost touched a private part of her body.

Then he would whisper to her, "Are you, all right?" The pastor would lean over and whisper to her, "remember I can still send the angels out to kill your family." Anita knew what that meant. She could not tell anyone what he did to her in the movie theater. Anita hated him and reconsidered her stand on having the gang take him out. When Anita arrived home, her mother would ask how everything went. Anita never answered. Her mother thought she was being rude and disrespectful and began to scold her. Anita was hoping by not answering her mother that she would know that something was wrong. She remembered what the pastor said about killing her family if she ever told. Anita began to hate God, male preachers and going to church. She could not understand why the pastor targeted her. Anita's behavior in the church was not flirtatious, and she did not dress seductively. The question kept coming into her mind, 'Why me?" Anita took out her frustrations on the kids in her school. She began fighting more and more in school. The teacher was sending letters home increasingly. Anita began talking back to her parents, which was suicidal. Her parents were from the deep South and believed in corporal punishment. Anita found herself being beaten with a belt by her father more often than she could count.

One day her mother asked her a question, and Anita flew in her mother's face with a nasty attitude as she so often did with those she was about to engage in a fight with at school. Her mother was angry, hurt, and surprised at her daughter's disrespectful behavior. Anita's mother, before she knew it, gripped her hands around Anita's throat and began choking her. With tears streaming down Anita's mother's face, she said to her daughter, "I brought you into this world, and I will take you out! How dare you jump in my face to fight me, I am you mother! I am not some kid you fight in the streets." By this time, Anita's father who was in the kitchen heard the commotion and went to see what was going on. He found his wife choking their daughter almost lifeless. Anita's father had to pry his wife's hand from around their daughter's throat. Her mother began hysterically to tell the father what Anita did to her. Anita's father took off his belt and began to beat her with it. Anita began to hate both of her parents. She went from a student receiving all A's in school to a student receiving C and D grades. The teacher requested a conference with her parents. She wanted to know if there was a problem at home. The teacher was concerned with Anita's behavior in class, her lack of attention, and interest she demonstrated towards her school work.

Anita's parents went home and sat her down and had a nice long talk with her. Her father wanted to beat her with his belt. However, the mother was against it. She was concerned and worried about her daughter. Anita was exemplifying behavior which suggested something was desperately wrong. Anita's mom wanted her to tell them what was wrong. Sitting in the presence of her parents, Anita broke out in sobbing tears and rage. She began to break and throw things around and screamed, "God why? God, why?" Her mother knew for sure something was wrong. Her mother grabbed her and began to hug her. She repeatedly spoke to her daughter in a soft tone, "We love you! We love you!" Anita's father began to cry. He felt that his daughter had a mental illness. His mind reflected on his mother who was in a mental institution for mental illness. He thought his daughter had inherited a mental condition from his mother. Anita's mother, a woman of God, knew that her daughter did not have a mental illness. Anita's father went to church only on Easter and Father's Day. His faith and belief in God were not as strong as his wife's faith. Anita finally calmed down. She still was afraid to tell her parents what was going on with her. Anita's mother later that night telephoned her pastor and told him everything that took place in their home that night. The pastor suggested that Anita do some office work for him. He said to her mother that he loved Anita like his daughter.

The pastor shared a similar situation with her concerning one of his daughters. He said that his daughter was hiding the fact that some kids were threatening her and taking money from her at knifepoint. The pastor told Anita's mother that he and his wife kept her away from that environment as much as they possibly could. The pastor said that he made unexpected visits to the school and he picked up his daughter every day after school. The pastor also stated how he gave his daughter a job working for him in the office as his personal secretary and how that took her mind off things as well as helped her get back on track. He suggested to Anita's mother to let Anita come and work for him, four hours on Saturdays. The pastor stated that it would be just the two of them and that maybe she would open up to him. He said children sometimes are more comfortable opening up to a non-family member rather than to a family member. Anita's mother thought that was a great idea. She talked it over with her husband. However, her husband had an uneasy feeling concerning his daughter being alone with a man for four hours, even if it was the pastor. Finally, Anita's mother talked him into it. Anita's mother excitedly told Anita what her new schedule would be on Saturdays. Anita began to cry and plead with her mother not to make her go. She promised her mother that she would do anything or act however her mother wanted her to if she would not make her take the job.

Anita's mother disregarded what her daughter's request. She told Anita that it was for her own good and that Anita had to give it a try. Anita begged God to let her die because she knew exactly, what the pastor had installed for her. Anita knew she would be alone and no one would be there to help her if she needed it. When Saturday morning came, Anita's mother took her to the church to meet with the pastor. They arrived at 10:00 a.m. and found the pastor sitting behind his desk in his study preparing Sunday's message. When he saw them, he got up and greeted them both. The pastor began to explain to Anita in the presence of her mother, exactly what she would be doing. He had a pile of papers that needed to be filed away. The pastor did a few as to show her how he wanted the work done. He told Anita she could also do some dusting. The pastor made an offer to pay her thirty dollars a Saturday for coming in. Her mother thought thirty dollars was a bit much to pay a thirteen-year-old for just filing some papers and dusting. However, the pastor insisted, and her mother accepted. Anita's mother kissed her and told her that she would be back to pick her up in four hours and she left her alone with the pastor. Anita was frightened, but the pastor suggested that she get started filing.

Anita was filing papers for about twenty minutes, while the pastor was supposedly preparing his Sunday sermon. The pastor appeared to be deeply into preparing his sermon and not paying any attention to her. Therefore, Anita began to relax and continue to file papers. However, the pastor was watching her all along when she was not looking. When he detected she was relaxed, he made his move. While Anita had her back turned to him filing, the pastor put on a condom. He got up from behind his desk quietly and went and stood behind her. The pastor began massaging her shoulders and telling her how pretty she was. Anita was scared. It seemed as if she could hear her heart beating. The pastor turned Anita around to face him. The pastor's genital area was exposed to her, and she began to cry bitterly. He began to touch Anita's chest area, and she started to fight him and push his hands away. The pastor grabbed her and forced her to the floor. With one hand, he pinned both of hers down and placed his heavy body of over two hundred pounds upon this thirteen-year-old girl weighing seventy pounds. At that time, Anita's mother was almost home when she remembered that she had not given Anita money for lunch. She knew the pastor would buy her daughter lunch. However, her husband had a problem with anyone buying his kids anything. Therefore, to keep the peace at home, she turned around and proceeded back to the church.

By this time, the Pastor had torn off Anita's undergarment and was in the process of raping the thirteen-year-old girl. Anita was screaming and crying bitterly. Her mother entered the church and heard her daughter screaming. She ran to the pastor's study and opened the doors and found the pastor on top of her daughter. Anita's mother began screaming, and shouting "get off my daughter." She picked up a lamp and knocked the pastor out with it. Anita's mother pushed him off of her daughter. Anita's mother helped her traumatized daughter up from the floor. She helped Anita put on her coat, and they quickly left the church building. Anita's mother did not call the police. She just wanted to get Anita out of there. Finally, she got Anita home. Anita was still traumatized and sore with bruises between her legs. Her mother was afraid to tell Anita's father because she knew that he would blame her for what happened. Anita's mother also knew that her husband would take the unregistered handgun he had and kill the preacher if he was not already dead. She also knew that her husband would kill her as well. Anita's mother begged her daughter not to tell anyone what had happened to her in the pastor's office. She explained to Anita that people would look at her funny and may treat her differently. Anita's mother did not realize how emotionally and mentally damaged her daughter was from the incident.

Anita felt violated, unclean and that somehow, she was the blame for what happened to her in the pastor's study. That man had seen parts of her body that Anita only wanted a husband to see. Anita's mother did not attend church services the following Sunday after the incident. Her husband asked why she and the children were not going to attend church services that Sunday. Anita's mother told her husband that Anita was not feeling well and she was going to stay home with their daughter. Anita's father asked her mother what was exactly wrong with Anita. Her mother replied, 'It is a girl thing." Her father assumed it was female problems and didn't pursue any further questioning his wife. The following week Anita went on a suicide mission. Anita's first attempt was to stab herself in the chest, but she could not bring herself to push the knife into her chest. In Anita's second attempt to commit suicide, she swallowed 250 pain pills. However, God had a plan for Anita's life, and he was not ready for her yet. She woke up the next day as if she had not taken anything at all. Anita grew very angry with God and began to curse him. She wanted to provoke God to kill her. Anita kept asking God repeatedly to let her die. The following Saturday her father noticed that her mother did not take Anita to the church to file papers for the pastor. When the father questioned his wife, she answered, "Anita is not feeling good, and that filing papers for the pastor was not such a good idea after all."

The third suicide attempt was made the following Saturday after the incident in the pastor's study. Anita stood outside on her brother's window ledge on the sixth floor of their six-story housing development. She went to leap to her death when something very extraordinary happened. As she began to move her body from the building to leap, an invisible arm formed around her waist, interrupting the jump. Anita saw no one, but she felt the arm embracing her on that window ledge, pushing her body back against the building. Anita did not understand what was happening to her. She was standing on a narrow window ledge six stories up not holding on to anything, why hadn't she fallen to the ground already? Anita thought, she should be dead now on the pavement. God began to speak audibly to Anita while she was standing on that ledge. He told her how much he loved her and for her to go back inside. Anita began to sob bitterly asking God, "How can you love me when your preacher tried to rape me, and you allowed it?" Anita began to tell God he did not love her, and if he did, he would have let her die. Meanwhile, Anita's parents along with the rest of the children were in the living room watching television. The last time her parents looked in on her, Anita appeared to be sleeping peacefully in her bedroom. Suddenly there was a knock at the door. It was a neighbor who saw Anita standing on the ledge. The concerned neighbor told Anita's parents that their daughter was standing on the window ledge. Her parents ran frantically to the bedroom where she was standing outside on the window ledge.

Her mother begged her not to jump, as her father reached out and pulled her back inside. Anita's father kept questioning her mother until she finally broke down and told him what had happened at the church the previous Saturday. In a rage, her father ran in the room and got the unregistered handgun from a locked fireproof box. He swiftly went by his wife and out the door. He got in his car and headed towards the church. The pastor was in his study, and it was the deacon's Saturday to clean the church. Therefore they were all there in full force. Suddenly Anita's father burst through the church doors using profanity looking for the pastor. Normally he had respect for God's house, but not this time. The deacons tried to stop him, but when he pulled out his gun, they backed up. Anita's father asked one of the deacons where was the pastor's study, and he pointed to where it was located. Anita's father burst into the study with the gun. He proceeded to where the pastor was sitting. The deacon aiding the pastor backed away from the pastor. Anita's father took the gun and placed the barrel on the pastor's genitals. Her father told the pastor that since he did not know what to do with what God had given him, that he should blow them off. Anita's father began to ask him "what kind of a sick man tries to rape a thirteen-year-old girl." Her father began to cry and said: "I use to believe in you and I use to believe in God." Anita's father went on to say, "but now I know there is no God. If he existed where was he when you were trying to rape my daughter?" Anita's father stated, "my wife swore to me up and down that my daughter would be safe with you." Anita's father said to the pastor, "Reverend I am about to send your soul to hell, and you will never misuse what you were born with ever again!" At this time, the deacons that were cleaning the church had walked into the pastor's study and heard everything that Anita's father said. They looked for the pastor to deny the accusations, but the pastor said nothing in his defense. With the revolver's barrel resting on his genitals, the pastor began to cry. He said nothing. The pastor's evasive behavior disturbed the deacons. It was not the first time an accusation of this nature was brought against the pastor. The last victim was a seventeen-year-old boy with autism. His mother left the church after bringing the matter before the deacons and church board members, which did not believe her accusation against the pastor. The young boy had a history of not telling the truth, and therefore no one took him seriously. However, this time the deacons believed their pastor was guilty as charged. There were too many holes in his story about the alleged church robbery where he supposedly got hit on the head with a lamp. While one of the deacons was pleading with Anita's father not to shoot the pastor's genitals off, another deacon called the police. Anita's father was now in a rage-blinded by his tears was about to pull back on the trigger of the handgun. At that time, his wife came in crying, begging him not to do it. She had called a female minister from the church and told her what had happened. The female minister rushed over and took Anita and her mother to the church.

Anita's mother left her sisters and brothers with a neighbor in the building who also belonged to the same church. Anita's mother kept pleading with her husband not to shoot the pastor. By this time, the police had arrived on the scene, and they were able to persuade Anita's father to put down the gun. A female officer took a statement from Anita and her mother as to what happened the previous Saturday. The pastor still said nothing in his defense. The pastor's wife had arrived at the church with three of their adult children. One of the deacons called her after calling the police. The pastor was arrested for child molestation and attempted rape. A female officer suggested that Anita is taken to the hospital, even though the attack occurred the Saturday before. Anita was taken to the hospital. When the female doctor examined her, she found scarring that proved that there was an attempt to force entry sexually. The pastor was sent to prison for his actions. The pastor's family in shame left the state and relocated to another state. Although the pastor was sent to prison for his actions, Anita's mother blamed the church board for not taking action against the pastor the first time an accusation was made against him. Anita's father became an atheist. Anita gave her life to Jesus two months later at a New Year's Eve church service. Anita promised God that if he saved her and used her for his glory, that she would make sure that no other preacher would do to any child what she experienced. God granted her request.

Anita still had to face being part of a gang. She wanted out but did not know how she was going to detach from the gang. After accepting Jesus into her life, Anita found the boldness and courage to talk to her mother about her gang activities. Anita also discussed with her mother the horrible things she did to prove that she was loyal to her gang. Anita expressed to her mother that the only way out of the gang was death. Anita thought her mother would be upset with her after hearing about her past activities. Instead to her surprise, Anita's mother was not. Her mother knew Anita was involved in something, but she could not pinpoint what it was. Anita's mother listened attentively to her daughter, as her heart began to sink. Her mother realized that her daughter's life was in danger, and they would need a miracle from God to get Anita out of this situation. Anita's mother began to explain to her daughter that God specialized in the impossible and that all things were possible with him. She also began to tell Anita about the concept of fasting and praying. Anita's mother told her that there were times that some things only come by prayer and fasting. She opened her Bible to [**St. Matthew 17:20-21**], to back up her statement.

Anita's mother turned her Bible to [**St. Matthew 6:16-18**], which explains the proper way to fast. After Anita had read both passages of scriptures with her mother, they both got on their knees and began to ask God's help and guidance concerning this situation. God spoke to Anita's mother while they were on their knees. He instructed them to enter an absolute fast for three days and nights, not ingesting anything, not even water. God also instructed them to pray for the gang members that they will open their hearts and receive Jesus Christ as their personal savior. Anita's mother asked God when exactly they should begin the fast. God told her that they should start the fast that night. Anita's mother prayed that God would touch and condition her husband's heart to accept the fact that she would be fasting, and therefore would not be intimate with him for the next three nights. When engaging in a spiritual fast one cannot be intimate with their mates [**1 Corinthians 7:5**]. When Anita's mother went to her father with this information, he did not argue with her. Anita's father reaction surprised her mother because she knew her husband had become an atheist after the incident with the pastor. Anita and her mother began a fast at eight o'clock p.m. the following Thursday night.

It was difficult for Anita the next day in school not eating or drinking anything, but she stayed on the fast. It was during recess that her gang cronies notice she was acting a bit strange. Anita seemed more distant than usual. Since Anita gave her life to Jesus, she always seemed somewhat distracted when the gang members came around her. This time her distraction was different. One of the leaders approached Anita and asked what was up with her? Anita just looked at her and smiled. Anita's body was weak from her first day of fasting, and she prayed that there would not be any physical altercations. The female gang leader came and stood in her face and demanded an explanation for her seemingly distant attitude. Anita stood expressionless while she prayed within for God's help. The female gang leader was about to hit her when the school security guard intercepted the punch. The school security guard asked the female gang member to leave the school grounds. She had entered the grounds illegally. Most of the gang members were high school students, who often came to the junior high school illegally to recruit members for the gang. Anita made it home unharmed that day. She found her mother, as usual, praying for the safe return of her children. When the last child had arrived home, Anita took her mother aside and told her what had happened to her in school. Anita and her mother began to praise God for keeping her safe. Anita and her mother had grown very close since she gave her life to Jesus.

The third day of the fast had ended on the following Sunday. Anita's body was physically weak, however, spiritually she felt rejuvenated. Her mother's body was strong physically and spiritually. She was accustomed to fasting absolutely without anything. God moved in an unusual way during the Sunday morning service. The presence of God filled the sanctuary. The believers were praising God in such a great magnitude until the church began to look foggy or hazy inside. Later Anita learned that the foggy or hazy appearance she saw was the glory of God. Anita was sitting down in the pews praising God when she felt something like electricity enter her toes. She could feel this electrical charge moving up her legs, and it continued upward through her whole body. When it reached her mouth, she began to speak in this language she could not understand. Her tongue was going, and she had no control over it. God had filled Anita with the baptism of the Holy Ghost, and she was speaking in an unknown language. After morning service, Anita's mother had embraced her and began to praise God with her daughter thanking God for his precious gift. Later that evening at eight o'clock, Anita and her mother prayed out of their fast. She and her mom did not partake of the Sunday dinner that was prepared for the rest of the family. Instead, they had soup, applesauce, fruit juice and water.

Their regimens consisted of soft foods because they had not eaten for three days. The following Monday Anita returned to school. She was wondering what action God had taken concerning her circumstances over the weekend. Anita was surprised to learn that the female gang leader

Patricia Baskerville

who threatened her, over the weekend had gotten arrested for pulling a gun on a woman. The criminal act was not the female gang leader's first offense, and she had a rap sheet a mile long. This female gang leader was always in and out of juvenile correctional institutions. This time she was going away for a long time. The female gang leader was being tried as an adult because she had a firearm in her possession. The battle seemed to be over. However, it was just beginning. Anita had another battle that she would fight. The battle Anita would experience is trusting in male pastors again. Anita did not realize this problem existed so strongly in her life and how it would later result as a great hindrance to her in ministry. The new church she and her family joined had a female pastor. Anita did not hate male pastors, but she never wanted to sit under another one as long as she lived. Anita found it very hard to bond with any male pastor. Anita was not open or receptive to them as she was to female pastors. Anita needed God to heal her in this area of her life, and no one recognized this problem, not even Anita.

A special note to the reader

God has many gifted men and women of God who are doing a great work for him. A person's gift does not always depict their walk with God. There are great preachers, prophets, prophetesses, and teachers within the body of Christ. Just because they lay hands on the sick, prophesy accurately, speak in tongues, dance in the spirit, preach or teach, it does not mean they are in right standing with God. It is going to be some

gifted people rejected by God and will end up in hell for all eternity [St. Matthew 7:22-23]. God is going to confess he never knew these people who do great works publicly and live a sinful life secretly. For this purpose, we must always keep our eyes on God. No one is above sinning. Respect the men and women of God but never put them in a category of being perfect.

A holy life publicly and privately is more impressive than any number of spiritual gifting. There was only one person who ever walked this earth in perfection, and his name is Jesus. Readers do not be impressed with anyone's gifts or how God uses an individual, but be impressed by the life that is lived behind the gifts! Parents, please educate your children concerning the limited powers God has given to humans. PLEASE make your children aware of the fact that God does not and will not give any human being permission to HURT or TOUCH another person SEXUALLY or pertaining to SEX in any way!

CHAPTER 2

Exciting New Levels

It was three months into the New Year since Anita gave her life to Jesus. She was about to experience levels in God beyond her wildest imagination. Anita's attitude towards fighting changed somewhat, but not completely. God had taken the fighting and warrior spirit she had possessed while being a gang member and used it for his glory. Anita no longer desired to fight other people. Instead, her desire was to fight the devil and everything that was evil. Anita wanted the devil to pay for everything he did to her and others. She knew her weapon was the word of God and that it was imperative that she learned how to use it. Anita's fourteenth birthday was only a month away. Her interests changed drastically. Anita engulfed herself with learning the Bible. She was not interested in watching television or playing outside. (It is nothing wrong with watching television and playing outside if you are a Christian youth). It was Anita's choice to read the Bible every chance she got. If she was not reading the Bible, she could always be found on her knees praying. Anita's mother knew she loved the Lord, but there were times she wondered if her daughter was taking things a bit to the extreme.

Anita had a desire to pray all night, every night. Her mother would not hear of her being on her knees all night, especially when she had school the next day. However, that did not stop Anita. She went to bed as instructed, but she did not go to sleep. Anita would lie awake all night long praying and talking to God. She would always fall asleep two hours before it was time for her to get up for school. Anita did this every night, all through high school. She never felt tired or sleepy during the day. Anita's hunger for more of God in her life was out of control like a brush fire. There was no stopping her. Her favorite passage of scripture was [St. John 14:12]. It was also her goal in God to have this passage of scripture exhibit in her life. Anita's father was disturbed by his daughter's behavior. Every time he passed by her bedroom, his daughter would be on her knees crying out to God to save or heal someone. One-day Anita's father interrupted her and threatened to put Anita in a home for girls if she did not stop praying so much. That did not stop her, Anita continued to pray. When her father saw that his threats did not move her, he began to say very painful things to his daughter. Anita's father told her one day how he would be glad when she reached a certain age so that he would be able to throw her out of his house.

Anita's father also told her it was not normal for a teenager to be praying all the time. He also said to her, "You are no longer my daughter and that he only has three daughters now." Her father's words were a painful blow to Anita. She had spent the prior years of her life trying to make her father proud of her. Anita had always longed for her father's acceptance and spent previous years trying to get it. Her father from that time on lavished her other sisters with his love and treated Anita with coldness. However, despite the emotional blow she received from her father, Anita kept on praying and reading the Bible. She asked God to be her father since her father had denounced her. Anita's relationship with God grew stronger because of this. One week before Anita's fourteenth birthday she had an experience that would change her course in God forever. Anita was lying in bed praying as usual. It was two hours before she was to get up for school.

All of a sudden, she heard a loud laughter that echoed loudly throughout the entire bedroom. Anita saw no one, but a voice spoke loudly and said, "I HAVE MY WONDER WORKERS, I HAVE SOME OF GOD'S PEOPLE AND BEFORE IT IS ALL OVER I WILL HAVE ALL OF GOD'S PEOPLE." Anita could not believe she was awake and this was happening. She knew it was the voice of Satan. Anita replied without thinking, "You will never have me." Within an instant her body was paralyzed, she was only able to move her eyes to the side to see this hairy creature that had hair like a bear, ears like a goat, and a funny shaped head which had more than two eyes on its forehead. Anita was experiencing her first demonic encounter, and she had no idea of what she was supposed to do. Immediately it came to her mind that demons tremble at the name of Jesus. Anita tried to open her mouth to call Jesus, but her mouth would not open.

The devil began to laugh and say to her "Call him. I dare you to call him. You cannot call him. Call him!" Anita with tears in her eyes began to pray inside her heart as she asked God to help her. Anita began to speak to God inwardly. She told God how she loved him and had been trying to serve him all she knew how. Anita asked God if he was going to allow the devil to take her over like that. Meanwhile, Satan was still laughing.

Anita heard God speak back to her from within her mind. He said, "Call on the name of Jesus from your heart." As Anita called the name of Jesus from her heart, she could feel a surge of some sort moving up her throat to her mouth. When it reached her mouth, she yelled "JESUS" loudly! The hairy beast that was trying to enter in her side flew out of her side with such force it hit the adjoining wall to her brother's room. The loud sound woke up her little sister in the bed next to her. Anita's little sister woke up and said to her with sleepy eyes, "Who hit the wall like that." Anita knew without a doubt that she was not sleeping. She went into the kitchen trembling and found her mother preparing her other little sister for school while making breakfast at the same time. When Anita's mother listened to what had happened to her daughter, she knew that God was going to use Anita greatly in the supernatural. Anita's mother explained to her that she had experienced her first demonic encounter. Her mother also told her that God was going to use her early in ministry and that she would be casting demons out of people as part of her ministry. Anita did not know if she should rejoice or be afraid.

One week after Anita's fourteenth birthday, a friend came to their home to spend the night. She was a married woman who had accepted Jesus as her Lord and Savior. However, her husband was not in agreement with her new lifestyle and had become somewhat abusive. The woman whom we will call (sister Hurricane) came to Anita's parent's home late on a Friday night. Anita's mother had compassion for the woman and put her up in her son's bedroom for the night. Her mother made up the sofa for Anita's brother to sleep in the living room. Normally no children were allowed in the living room unless the entire family was watching television together, which usually was on the weekends only. Every bedroom had a television in it. The following Saturday morning Anita's mother made breakfast for the entire family. Anita's younger siblings wolfed down their breakfast quickly and rushed off to watch Saturday morning cartoons. Her father went off to work. Anita was left at the table alone with her mother and their houseguest. God began to show Anita in the spirit a hideous spirit inside of the woman. At one instance when the woman looked at Anita a chill went down Anita's back. Not knowing what to do about what she saw, Anita began to pray within asking God's guidance as to what he wanted her to do. Sister Hurricane finally spoke and said to Anita, "God is showing you something about me. What is it? Anita was hesitant to say what she saw. Finally, she said, "God is showing me a spirit binds you."

At that time, God spoke to Anita and told her it was a witchcraft spirit. God showed Anita in an open vision the neighbor who was responsible for this. He showed Anita the decorum of this woman's home, whom she had never visited before. Sister Hurricane, in shock and fear, was surprised at the accurate words that came out of Anita's mouth. God instructed Anita to pray for the woman, but she was not to lay her hands anywhere on this woman's body. She was to just point her hand towards the woman and pray. Anita, her mother, and sister Hurricane went into the living room to pray. God gave Anita the words to say. Surprisingly, she was not afraid. God told Anita to say these words, "In the name of Jesus, you foul witchcraft demon I command you in Jesus name to come out of this body and return to the pit of hell from which you came!" Sister Hurricane fell to the floor, and her head looked as if it was going to fold back under her back. God told Anita to say these words, "In the name of Jesus you foul witchcraft demon you will exit now and not destroy the body of this woman as you exit. In the name of Jesus come out of her now!" Sister Hurricane looked as if she vomited something out of her mouth.

God showed Anita in the spirit when the witchcraft spirit left. Anita also saw in the spirit how the demon exited out of the woman's mouth. It exploded like a balloon as it exited in the spirit and left a black liquid substance behind in the physical. Sister Hurricane opened her eyes as she was still lying on the living room floor. Coming out of both sides of her mouth was saliva that was black as tar, and her tongue was coated with something that looked like black liquid tar. Anita asked sister Hurricane to stand up and look at her tongue in the mirror hanging on the wall in the living room. When sister Hurricane stood up and looked at herself in the mirror, she screamed with fear. Anita explained to her that the demon had left, and what she saw was proof that a demon was in her and did exit through her mouth. Anita instructed her to go to the bathroom and rinse her mouth with clear water, and the black substance will go away. Sister Hurricane did what Anita said, and it went away. The strangest thing happened when she rinsed her mouth; her spittle was not black but clear. Anita had cast out her first demon at the age of fourteen. Her battles from that time until the present always consisted of demonic warfare; casting out demons either in face-to-face prayer or binding them during intercessory warfare prayer.

Anita went into the hospital praying for the sick. Her pastor at first thought she was too young to receive a missionary card to go into the hospitals. The pastor told Anita she was free to visit the hospitals and pray for the sick, but she was not going to give her a missionary card to do so; therefore, she was not given one at first. That did not stop Anita. She found hospitals that did not require a visitor's pass during visiting hours, and she would visit those hospitals praying for the sick. Anita arrived at these hospitals before visiting hours and would sit patiently in the lobby. While waiting she would ask God what ward should she visit that day? Anita would always have an answer by the time visiting hours began. The fourteen-year-old walked the hospital ward that God instructed her to enter with her Bible in her hands and a smile on her face. God also instructed her how to minister in the hospitals. Anita would walk to each bed, speaking just above a whisper introducing herself to the patient. Anita would then ask if they would like prayer. If the answer was yes, she prayed very softly above a whisper. If the answer was no, she smiled and told them that Jesus loved them and have a nice day. Anita would move from bed to bed until she had covered the entire ward. However, not many people refused her. They would always ask her age and would be inspired by the teenager's love for God and the zeal she carried to win souls. Anita graduated from the eighth grade with honors.

The marking period she had fallen back in her grades due to the incident with the pastor, God gave her favor with her teachers and only her high-grade scores were recognized. Anita spent the entire summer praying for people in the hospital. As she went back, she received testimonies from the patients, and some of the nurses of healings from diabetes, asthma, hypertension, and scheduled surgeries that were canceled. Anita took down people's names as she prayed for them. She added them to her prayer list at home, which looked like a little book. Anita took much opposition from older Christians and ministers who felt she was too young and didn't know what she was doing. Her female pastor was no exception. Anita exhibited great knowledge of God's word. When called upon to explain a verse from the Bible, Anita explained it so simplistically that a small child could follow and understand her. Some of the Christians and ministers in her church were jealous of the simplistic revelations and knowledge God gave Anita to teach and preach his word. With much resistance from her pastor, Anita was ordained an Evangelist at the age of fifteen. She was not looking for a title or position in the church she just wanted to win souls. However, nothing could stop her from ministering in the hospitals or standing on street corners telling individuals that passed her that Jesus loved them.

Sometimes a person would stop with tears in their eyes and say to Anita, "Young lady do you know that I needed to hear that!" Anita did not wait on anyone to go with her to minister. She took Jesus and off she went to witness in the streets. Sometimes she would be walking past a supermarket, and God would tell her to go inside. God would instruct her to go down a certain aisle and go up to a person and tell them that Jesus loved them. Anita obeyed God. Sometimes it was received at that moment. Other times it was not. Nevertheless, she obeyed God. Anita learned from experience that a person might not receive God's word at that moment. However, somewhere down the line when faced with a problem they will remember that a teenager came into the supermarket and told them that Jesus loved them. Some of the people she has told this to did not receive it at first, but later they remembered the words spoken to them by a young girl. As a result of this, they gave their lives to Jesus. For some people hearing that Jesus loves them made a difference between them taking their lives and accepting the life, Jesus has for them.

A note to the reader

No matter who and what age an individual may be, God can use them. Don't let age or people inside the church or outside of the church, discourage you

from going after the things of God, or winning souls for him. Perhaps family members may have forsaken you or turned their backs on you because of your relationship with God. Be encouraged; you are not alone! God let us know that he will be a parent to us if they forsake us [Psalm 27:10].

CHAPTER 3

High School

Anita enters high school not knowing what to expect. She wondered if there were any other Christians in the school beside herself. Anita had no idea that she was about to experience another new and exciting level in God. High School was different from Jr. High School. In Jr. High School Anita had the same people in all of her classes. In High School, Anita had different people in all her classes including homeroom. However, there was one exception, which was part of God's Divine plan. There was a young girl in all her classes which we will call (Grace). Grace was a "five percenter." A "five percenter" was a spin-off group from the Muslim religion. Their women were referred to as "earth" and the men as "gods." The "five percenter" was a popular group in the seventies and eighties. The girls wore their faces and heads covered, and a long dress with pants under them. Grace appeared not to be very friendly but kept a close eye on Anita. Anita finally met some more Christians attending the same school. They met for lunch every day within the cafeteria. Eating in a school cafeteria was also a new experience for Anita. She used to go home for lunch in Jr. High School because the school's location was a block away from her home. The High School was located on the other side of town, and it would be utterly impossible for her to go home for lunch every day. Anita enjoyed the school lunches. They were not prepackaged microwave foods. The lunches were cooked daily in the school's kitchen. It was like eating out at a restaurant for Anita. God was about to show himself to Anita in a mighty way.

Anita and her four siblings all came down with the chickenpox at the same time. Each of the children had to remain home for two weeks during the incubation period. When Anita returned to school, her English class was in the process of taking their midterms. A book was given to each child to read while Anita was home sick with the chickenpox. Ninety percent of the test was based on the book, and the other ten percent was on grammar. Upon returning to school Anita presented to all her teachers a copy of her doctor's note explaining her absence from school. All her teachers except for the English teacher were sympathetic and had agreed to give her time to prepare to take their midterm. Anita approached her English teacher to ask if she should take the midterm that day, thinking she was going to be allotted more time for preparation. Her English teacher was very rude and arrogant and insisted she take the test with the rest of the class. Anita reminded her that she was out of school sick. Therefore she was unable to get the book given to the rest of the class to prepare for the test. Her teacher was cold and expressionless.

Anita proceeded to ask if she got a failing grade on the test would it count. She knew she could not possibly write or answer questions about a book she had never read. Anita's teacher said very arrogantly, "yes it will count." She needed a miracle to pass this midterm. Anita could not afford to fail any classes. Her school was a trade high school that specialized in fashion designing. Within a trade high school, if an individual failed a class, it meant six months of extra time automatically added to the four years. Anita sat at her desk praying silently, asking God to help her. She did not know what she was going to do. Her English teacher passed out a blank legal-size sheet of paper. She instructed the class to write an essay on the book. Anita's English teacher also handed out a grammar worksheet, which required inserting the proper grammar word within the sentence. Anita proceeded to start the grammar sheet when God told her not to do that first. He instructed her to place the legal-size sheet of paper in front of her and pray with her eyes open. As Anita began to pray, God in an open vision began showing her pages of the book she was not given and had never read. God did not stop there! He gave Anita word for word what to write on her paper. Anita wrote a full-page essay on the book she had never read. She completed the grammar page and was finished with her test before time. The next day the papers were graded and handed back. Everyone was given his or her test papers back, except for Anita. The highest passing grade in the class so far was seventy percent. Anita's English teacher held her paper and asked to see her after class. After class, the students left the inside of the classroom. However, they congregated outside of the classroom door to see what kind of grade Anita had gotten. Some of the students were making sarcastic remarks about the church girl getting into trouble. Once the classroom was empty, her teacher asked her to come up to her desk. She proceeded to ask Anita repeatedly if she had ever read the book the class was given while she was home sick with the chickenpox. Anita continued to tell her teacher she had never set eyes on that book until she returned to school. Finally, her teacher gave her back her midterm paper. At the top of the page in red was written 95% Excellent. Anita had lost five points on the grammar sheet and not her essay. God had given her a miracle and the highest grade in the class. When she went into the school hallway, the students were hanging outside of the classroom door. They were all shocked to see the grade she had gotten, including Grace the "five percenter." At lunchtime, Anita shared her victorious testimony with the other Christians. They rejoiced with her and thanked God for a notable miracle manifesting. The young Christians were also encouraged to know that if God did it for Anita, surely, he could perform the same miracle for them.

One day a girl whom we will call Mercy approached Anita while she was standing in line to get lunch. The girl had heard what happened to Anita and wanted to question her. Mercy's mother was also a born again Christian. While Mercy was questioning Anita, God revealed to Anita that Mercy was a backslider, which is a person who once was a Christian and turned away from God. Anita interrupted her speaking and said to her, "God wants you to return to him. He loves you and wants you to come back to him." Mercy very arrogantly said, "I am having too much fun sinning." Anita replied, "I will pray for you." Mercy had no idea what she was about to experience. Anita went home and entered into intercessory prayer for Mercy at exactly 4:00 pm that afternoon. Meanwhile, Mercy was at home helping her mother in the kitchen. Exactly at the time when Anita was in prayer, Mercy's body began to tremble. She grabbed hold of the refrigerator so she would not fall to the floor. Mercy began to cry and ask what was happening to her. Mercy's mother said to her, "someone is praying a powerful prayer for you." Then Mercy's mother began to pray aloud and ask God to deal with her daughter. Mercy was not happy about what had just happened to her. She knew who was responsible and swore to make the person pay tomorrow at school.

The next day Anita was sitting with her Christian friends having lunch when Mercy rudely came and pushed her lunch tray away from her, seating herself in front of Anita on the cafeteria table. Mercy made a big scene, and therefore all eyes were on her and Anita. She got in Anita's face and asked her what she was doing approximately 4:00 p.m. the previous day. Anita boldly said, "I was praying for you." Mercy proceeded to tell her what had happened to her. Anita began rejoicing to know that God had heard her prayer and moved so quickly. Mercy did not think it was a rejoicing situation. She told Anita if she prayed for her again, that she would beat her up. Then she got in Anita's face and asked if she was going to pray for her again. Anita replied boldly, "Yes, I am going to pray for you again." Mercy said to Anita, "Are you crazy or something? I just threaten to beat you up, and you are still going to pray for me?" Anita replied, "I am going to continue to pray for you, and I do not mind saying a prayer right now!" She bowed her head, and the other Christians joined in as she began to pray silently for Mercy. When Anita opened her eyes, Mercy was gone, and all eyes were still on her. She casually reached for her lunch tray and continued her lunch and conversation with her friends. Mercy paid a heavy price for that performance she put on in the cafeteria. God takes it personally when you bother or hurt what belongs to him. There were some children in the Bible that called a man of God "bald head" [**1 Kings 2:23-24**] and were destroyed by two she bears. It is a dangerous thing to put your mouth or hands on God's property!

Mercy left school that day in the car of a married man whom with she was having an affair. Mercy was seventeen years old. Anita saw her getting into the car. God placed it on Anita's heart to begin praying for Mercy's life. The next day Anita was told that Mercy was in a bad car accident after school. She was told the accident was so bad that everyone in the car should have been killed. The driver who was the married man was in critical condition, and Mercy suffered some bruises and mild injuries. God was merciful because of the prayer Anita had prayed the previous afternoon. Mercy never returned to the school after that. Some friends of hers said that she was attending a high school closer to her home. God continued to perform miracles in school for Anita.

Grace the "five percenter" was observing Anita's life. Anita never witnessed to her verbally. One-day Grace approached Anita and told her that her mother was an Evangelist. She also told Anita that her mother had been trying to get her to go to church. Anita asked Grace if she was going to go. Grace replied that she did not believe in the things her mother did because she was an "Earth." Anita did not make a reply as to Grace's statement; she just smiled and said to Grace, have a nice weekend. Anita went home and travailed in prayer for Grace. She turned her plate down a few hours each day of the weekend for Grace.

On the following Monday morning, as Anita was putting her coat away in her locker, Grace walked in. Grace spoke to Anita, and she looked different. Grace's hair was uncovered and fixed nicely, she was wearing a dress without the pants under them, and she smiled at Anita when she spoke to her.

Anita was shocked at what she had seen and wondered if Grace had given her life to Jesus. At that moment, Grace approached Anita with a big smile on her face. Grace said to her excitedly, "Guess where I went yesterday?" Anita replied excitedly, "Tell me where you went yesterday?" Grace said," I went to church with my mother, and I gave my life to Jesus. God also filled me with the baptism of the Holy Ghost, speaking in tongues." Both girls forgot they were in school and began to praise God openly in the locker room. Then they embraced each other. Grace told Anita she had been watching the different miracles that

God! Where Were You?

God had performed for her. Grace also stated that she told her mother that there was a little preacher girl in all her classes. She told Anita each time something miraculous happened to her, she went home and told her mother. Grace's mother told her that she needed to hang around the little preacher girl and that maybe some of what she had would rub off on Grace. Many more souls were won for Jesus in High School.

There was a teacher who treated Anita badly in her junior year of High School. Anita prayed and fasted for that teacher over the summer that she would give her life to Jesus. The following school semester, the teacher was looking for Anita. When she found Anita, she asked her forgiveness for all the mean and nasty things she did to her. The teacher went on to tell Anita that over the summer she gave her life to Jesus. She asked God to allow her to see Anita so that she may apologize to her.

God continued to use Anita greatly. She had become a powerful preacher, teacher, and soul winner for Jesus by the time she graduated from High School. Anita graduated from High School with honors.

A note to the reader

Never let anyone discourage you from doing anything for God. Christianity is not only verbalized to others, but also in the life that you live before people. There is not a person too young or old for God to use him or her. God is looking for a willing vessel, and the age does not matter. Remember no one is too bad for God to change.

CHAPTER 4

A Different Kind of Life

Anita was out of High School and was about to experience a different kind of life. Anita had decided to work for a year and then go to college later. College required money, and her parents did not have much money. Anita received her first job at a Brokerage House. She was hired as a file clerk. Within three months God blessed her, and she was promoted to Cash Dividend Clerk. Anita was a very hard and conscientious worker. She never took extra breaks and never exceeded her lunch hour. She was taught in her church to work on your job as if working unto God. One evening after a Thursday night prayer service a young male minister from the church walked up to Anita and introduced himself. We will call him (Minister Blessing). Minister Blessing was a very tall and handsome young man. He was much taller than Anita. Her head stopped at his chest area. Minister Blessing was five years older than Anita. He had his home and had an excellent job working with government law enforcement. Minister Blessing was a sharp dresser and drove a very expensive car. He was also a powerful prophet and preacher. Every single woman in the church desired to be his wife. They were always in his face and trying to get him to take them some place in his car. Anita was different from the other women in the church. She tried to avoid being in Minister Blessing's path at any cost. The more Anita tried to avoid Minister Blessing, the more he pursued her. Finally, Anita agreed to go on a date with Minister Blessing. He took Anita to a quaint little Italian restaurant. After dinner Minister Blessing and Anita went for a romantic walk. Minister Blessing held Anita's hand as they walked slowly while discussing the ministry.

This was a new experience for Anita. She was a little uncomfortable holding this handsome gentleman's hand. However, she tried her best not to show it. They dated for six months steadily. Anita was hated and despised by many of the women in the church. Many of the women felt that they had more to offer Minister Blessing than Anita. Most of the women in her church owned their homes, owned their own business, or held high paying jobs. They wore expensive designer clothing. However, none of that mattered to Minister Blessing. He loved Anita, and he wanted to marry her. Minister Blessing felt that in whatever area in Anita's life she was lacking, that he would make up the difference. It did not matter if it was physical or spiritual. Minister Blessing and Anita often ministered together. They were powerful together in the pulpit. After six months of dating, Minister Blessing proposed marriage to

Anita. She accepted his proposal. Her family, especially Anita's father, loved Minister Blessing. Anita found this to be very strange, especially since her father became an atheist after the pastor incident that occurred when she was younger. A large wedding was planned. Meanwhile the enemy of our soul, the devil was at work. Women in the church began to approach Anita with disturbing information concerning Minister Blessing's past. They told her about the assorted affairs he had with them. The women in the church were hoping that what they told her would hurt Anita emotionally. The women hoped that Anita would break up with Minister Blessing so that they could have another crack at trying to get him to commit to them in marriage. God reminded Anita of the things in her past. She began to think of how she would feel if her past mistakes would be held against her. Therefore, Anita could not hold anything against the man of God concerning his past. Anita thanked God for reminding her of where she came from regarding her past. She almost lost out on receiving a blessing she felt was from God. She went to Minister Blessing and asked his forgiveness for wavering concerning their relationship. He forgave her, and now they were well on their way to holy matrimony.

A note to the reader

Never let rumors false or true deter you from the things or people of God. Beware of those who are so eager to bring bad news about someone or criticize others. Their goal is to make you turn away

from God's intended blessing. Beware of the hidden agendas, motives, and undertones that these people may have. Ask yourself a question, "How will the bearer of bad news benefit if you walk away from God's intended blessing?"

CHAPTER 5

The Marriage

Minister Blessing and Anita were married on Christmas Day of the same year they began dating. They had a beautiful wedding with a Cinderella theme. Anita felt that she was the most blessed woman on earth. Minister Blessing had a vacation villa in the mountains, where they spent their honeymoon. Anita was very nervous on her wedding night. She had never been with a man before. Minister Blessing, however, was not a gentleman on their wedding night. Anita had shared with him the horrors she experienced sexually at the age of thirteen at the hands of the man who was her pastor at that time. She felt that since he knew her history that he would be patient with her in the bedroom. Minister Blessing was not! When they reached the villa, Minister Blessing carried his bride over the threshold. They kissed as he proceeded to the bedroom carrying his bride. Once inside the bedroom, he placed her on the bed. Anita was still wearing her wedding dress. Minister Blessing began to undress. Anita then began to undress. She laid out on the bed a beautiful white negligee she had received at her bridal shower. Anita was about to go into the bathroom when her husband startled her, as he stood before her completely naked. He grabbed her and threw her on the bed. Minister Blessing then literally tore her wedding dress from her body. Then he began intimate acts resembling rape instead of love. Anita began to cry and ask him to stop. The more she cried, the rougher he became. Anita began to have flashbacks as to what happened to her in the pastor's office when she was thirteen years old. She began to fight her husband as if he was a rapist. The more she fought, the rougher he became. Anita was crying furiously. At that moment, she hated her husband just as much as she had hated the pastor at the age of thirteen when he tried to rape her. Anita's husband kept this up all night. There were moments that she wished she was dead. Anita did not enjoy her first night of intimacy with her husband. However, he was too selfish to notice.

Anita was an excellent housekeeper. She made every attempt to please her husband in and out of bed. Anita served her husband his meals in bed where she often fed him like a baby. She drew his bath for him and would take great pleasure in bathing him like a baby. After the bath, Anita would rub her husband's entire body with baby oil. Anita babied, spoiled, and cuddled her husband all the time. However, the treatment was not reciprocated. Regardless, Anita never stopped. She felt a mate was a precious gift from God and that all God-given gifts should be cherished. Anita loved to cook, and she was excellent at it. Everyday Minister Blessing came home to meals that most people prepared on Sundays. Anita took great pleasure and honor in doing things for her husband. She hoped and prayed that God would deal with Minister Blessing concerning the way he handled her in the bed. Anita wanted just once for him to be gentle with her so that she could enjoy him as much as he seemed to be enjoying her. She did not look forward to intimacy with her husband at all.

Minister Blessing also had a bad habit of talking about past sexual encounters with other women during intimacy. This did not help Anita's self-esteem at all. Anita always felt that she was in competition with the women of his past. She held the fear that Minister Blessing might leave her someday for one of them. Therefore, Anita began to do to him the things he said the other women did to him. She wanted to please him so badly. Anita lost her identity when she got married. Her entire life was wrapped around Minister Blessing, his wants, and needs. Minister Blessing and Anita conceived a baby after one year of marriage. When Anita became six months pregnant, Minister Blessing became temperamental. One-day Anita was playing around with him as she so often did on previous occasions. She stood in front of the television to get his attention while he was watching a football game. Anita often did this to get Minister Blessing's attention, and he would tickle her until she moved out of the way. On this particular day, his response was unpredictable. He got up and walked over to Anita. She thought he was going to tickle her as usual. Instead, he walked up to her and slammed her into a nearby wall, then punched her in her stomach, he then proceeded to slap her in the face repeatedly. Anita went into labor immediately. Minister Blessing's response to her was, "see what you made me do!" Anita was taken to the hospital by ambulance and was examined the doctors who noticed the bruise on her stomach and face. Minister Blessing was asked to leave, and the doctors privately asked Anita if she had received a blow to her stomach and if her husband had hit her in the face. She cried but never answered. Minister Blessing came back into the room. The doctors began to question him concerning the bruise on his wife's stomach and face. He denied knowing anything concerning the bruise. When the doctors left out of the room, he whispered in her ear that if she said anything, he would kill her.

Anita's labor pains severely increased. The monitor on her stomach showed that something was wrong with the baby. Anita gave birth to stillborn twin boys. The direct blow to her stomach caused the babies death. Once again, she was experiencing a private hell and could not tell anyone about it. Minister Blessing became colder towards her more each day. At this point intimacy with him was outright rape. He would rip her clothes from her anytime he felt like it and would roughly and forcefully have sexual intercourse with her. Minister Blessing had rough sex with her so often until she developed cysts in her vaginal area. As a result of this Anita had to have laser surgery to remove the cysts. Minister Blessing picked up Anita from the hospital and took her home. When Anita arrived home, all she could think about was lying down. Her vaginal area was sore from the minor operation. Minister

Blessing looked at his wife lying there on the bed. All of a sudden, he had a strong desire to have sex with her. Without warning, he climbed on top of his wife and began to have sexual intercourse with her roughly. Anita screamed in agony, as her stitches were being torn open. Blood was everywhere. Anita had to be taken back to the hospital to be stitched up again. A social worker came to see her. The social worker gave her a number to an organization for battered women. Instead, she contacted a close friend of hers from High School.

Her friend had left her husband years ago for trying to assault their two-year-old daughter, sexually. She and her daughter were living alone in hiding from her estranged husband. Her friend whom we will call (Sister Safe) came to the hospital to see her. Anita shared with her what her husband had done to her. Sister Safe offered Anita to stay with her for as long as she needed to. Anita accepted Sister Safe's offer to stay at her home. Sister Safe is one of Anita's friends that Minister Blessing had never met. He had only heard of her. Anita stayed with Sister Safe for three months. Meanwhile, she still attended the same church that Minister Blessing attended. At this point, Minister Blessing had given a very different version of what was happening at home. He portrayed himself as being the victim instead of the victimizer. Anita allowed the saints in the church to run a guilt trip on her for leaving her husband. As a result of this, she returned home to Minister Blessing and his abuse. Minister Blessing continued to rape her in bed. Anita cried many nights and asked God to take her home to be with him. She felt all alone. The

Saints did not seem to understand or want to understand. Anita's husband was raping her more frequently than before. Minister Blessing began watching porn movies. After watching the movies, he would forcefully have sex with his wife. Minister Blessing would become angry with her if she did not perform like the women in the movies.

During all this, Anita became pregnant once again. She was three months into the pregnancy when one-day Minister Blessing up and left her. Anita came home from work to find that he had moved out while she was at work. She was devastated on the one hand and relieved on the other side. Anita felt a sense of peace because she was carrying in her womb a little person that would love her unconditionally forever. However, that peace was short lived. On a Sunday night two weeks after Minister Blessing had left her, Anita began to experience sharp pains around her navel area. She felt as if she had to use the bathroom. When Anita sat on the toilet, she experienced an extremely sharp pain in her navel area. All of a sudden, she felt something drop out of her. Anita stood up to see what had dropped out of her. She saw a big lump that looked like raw liver. Anita realized at that time she miscarried her baby in the toilet. She went to the emergency room at a nearby hospital. It was confirmed that she was pregnant and had miscarried. Anita went into a deep state of depression. The saints in the church were no help. Some of the women were telling her she was better off not having a husband or child and that she could dedicate her life more to God being alone. Anita disagreed with them and resented them each time they made that statement to her. She always wanted to be a wife and a mother. Anita felt that people or things could only hinder you from the things of God if you allow them too!

A special note to the reader

Never put the blessings of God before God. Never love any creature more than the creator. Remember in every situation God has created a way of escape [1Corinthians 10:13]. Never allow the opinion of others to cause you to remain in a situation when God is giving you an out. We are given choices as well as a way out of something when God creates a way of escape. Recognize your way of escape and the choices you are given. There are times when God is telling us to disconnect or leave something or someone alone. Often we attribute this to the devil when we do not want to accept the way of escape God has provided. Readers accept God's way of escape out of situations that have become too much for you. It may save your life!

CHAPTER 6

Moving On

Anita remained alone for five years. She continued to preach the gospel. She had begun to travel from state to state preaching the gospel. Anita was very lonely. She still carried a torch for Minister Blessing. Not a day went by that Anita did not pray for his return. She had been asking God to put love back in his heart for her. Anita felt that she should be the bigger person; therefore, she began calling him at work. Minister Blessing would not accept any of her phone calls. Holidays were the hardest to get through. Anita dreaded Thanksgiving, Christmas, and New Years. She had often asked God what was next up the road for her. Anita knew that "All things work together for good to them that love God, to them who are the called according to his purpose," [**Roman 8:28**]. However, she could not possibly see or understand how all the hellish situations she had experience was working together for her good. To make matters worse, Minister Blessing married someone else without giving her a divorce. Anita found out this shocking news through the media. It appeared that wife number two was involved in some legal problems that resulted in violence. Minister Blessing being law enforcement official was given the call since it involved his wife. However, when he arrived on the scene, his behavior was not becoming of law enforcement official. Minister Blessing pulled his service revolver without probable cause.

The media had a field day with the footage of film they shot. Minister Blessing's job and career were on the line. His department had a very experienced and thorough attorney to protect their law enforcement officials. The attorney discovered two marriage licenses on file and no divorce document. This was brought to Minister Blessing's superior officer. His superior officer threatened him that if he did not produce a divorce document to void out one of the marriage licenses, he would put him in jail himself for bigamy. Minister Blessing began divorce proceedings against Anita. He was determined to have nothing more to do with her. Once the divorce papers were officially filed, he delivered the papers to Anita without warning. As a result of this Anita almost had a nervous breakdown. She became very angry with God. Anita began to entertain thoughts of death and not living for God anymore. She began to feel as if all her fasting and praying was in vain. Anita could not understand how something can be of God in one instance, and seemly be the worst mistake of your life in another. In a rebellious state, she began to date other men and did not care about the consequences. Anita began to dress more seductive. She was not thinking about looking holy. Anita wanted

Minister Blessing to regret his decision in divorcing her. She wanted him to desire her. Anita felt that the other woman must have been more alluring to him in her style of dress and mannerisms. Therefore, Anita began to loosen up more. She still wanted him back. This was dangerous because Anita felt the seductive old person she was at thirteen trying to resurface. Anita began to flirt with brothers in the church, giving the impression that she was easy. She hoped that her behavior would somehow get back to Minister Blessing. At this time, Minister Blessing and his second wife had joined another church.

Anita had met another minister. This minister's standard of holy living was not biblical. He believed in heavy petting and premarital sex. This minister told Anita he always tried on his shoes first before he bought them. Anita came very close to falling into a sinful relationship with this minister. She often found herself fantasizing about being with him sexually. When Anita came to herself, she was so out of sync with God until she needed help and someone to talk to before she got herself any deeper in trouble. Her flesh was out of control, and all she could think about was how badly she wanted to satisfy it. Unfortunately, there was no one that she could talk to about her situation. Speaking to anyone about her problem would mean being blackballed from her church or position. Like so many believers today, she held on to her position and status in the church, hoping that no one would find out her secret. Anita found it harder and harder to resist the opposite sex when approached with sexual undertones. She would cry and beg God to take away the desire to have sex. It seemed the more she prayed, the greater her appetite became for sex. Finally, she went on a fast. Anita asked God to help her and deliver her. She told God that she did not want to sin, but the desire seemed to be getting stronger than her will. After the fast, Anita seemed to be okay. However, she met a man whom we will call (Deacon Brown Eyes). He was an extremely handsome man. Deacon Brown Eyes fell in love with Anita at first sight. He told her he did not believe in sex before marriage.

Deacon Brown Eyes also told her constantly that she was beautiful. They dated for two years. Their relationship was strictly platonic. After two years of dating, Deacon Brown Eyes asked Anita to marry him. Anita had grown to love Deacon Brown Eyes. However, the church she attended did not believe in second marriages. Deacon Brown Eyes was a member of a church that did believe in second marriages. Anita prayed to God about the marriage. Unfortunately, she did not wait for an answer. God went to great lengths to tell Anita WAIT! All Anita could think about was finally having someone in her life again. She had missed babying, pampering, and spoiling a man. Anita realized that if she went through with this marriage, she would lose many friends. She also realized most painful of all; she would have to leave her church. Anita took a chance in her church. She went to her pastor and told him she was engaged to be married again. Anita's pastor was not happy to hear this news. He explained to her that her license to preach would be taken back if she proceeded with this marriage. Anita questioned her pastor as to why her license would be revoked. Her pastor told her that she was going to hell if she remarried again. Anita begged God to forgive her for what she was about to do. She felt that for her to make a good soldier for God, it would be better if she married. She did not want to sin, and she had begun to have trouble in her flesh. Anita married Deacon Brown Eyes. As her pastor had promised, her license to preach in the church was revoked.

Anita began attending the church Deacon Brown Eyes was attending. One year into the marriage Anita conceived and gave birth to a boy. Anita almost died in childbirth. Her heart had stopped during the delivery process, and her blood pressure was almost near two hundred over one hundred. On top of all her problems, she had toxemia. After the birth of her son, things could not have seemed better for Anita. However, all that was about to change. Six months after the birth of their son, Deacon Brown Eyes decided he did not want to sleep in the bedroom anymore with Anita. Anita would find herself begging her husband to make love to her. She would often find him watching pornography movies and satisfying himself sexually. Once again Anita was faced with a situation that she could not tell anyone. She bought sexy nightgowns, wore her long hair down and wore his favorite perfume. Anita was determined to seduce her husband. However, her husband did not acknowledge all her attempts. Anita never thought that she would be married and burning in her flesh. Deacon Brown Eyes was another sexual abuser. He did not rape Anita as Minister Blessing had done on several occasions. Instead, Deacon Brown Eyes would wait until Anita was asleep or on her knees praying and he would cover her with semen. He would stand over her and relieve himself sexually covering her body with semen. One day in a rage of anger, Deacon Brown Eyes punched their one-year-old son in the eye while Anita was at work. He also cut up all their furniture with a razor. When Anita arrived home and saw what he had done, she called the police. Deacon Brown Eyes was arrested and had to attend parenting classes and anger management classes. However, this did not stop Deacon Brown Eyes from going into a rage about anything. If a clerk shortchanged him at the store, he would come home and rip the doors and cabinets from the hinges. Deacon Brown Eyes often punched holes in the wall, grazing Anita's head.

The worse was not over for Anita. Her father died. Anita and her father were not very close. Her father had disowned her when she accepted Jesus into her life. Despite Anita's best efforts to have a daughter father relationship, her father would not give an inch. She mourned her father's death differently than her other siblings. Anita wept at her father's casket profusely. She was wondering if the man who once occupied that body ever loved her. Anita sought consoling from her husband. Unfortunately, she did not get it. Deacon Brown Eyes did not sit with her at the funeral, and he did not stand with her at the cemetery. One week after Anita's father was buried Deacon Brown Eyes packed up his bags went back home to live with his mother. Anita asked him why he was packing to leave. Deacon Brown Eyes' response was, "I am better off with my mother." This, of course, devastated Anita. She had a child to bring up by herself. Anita felt God wanted her to move away. Therefore, she went on a six-day absolute fast. A fast where nothing is ingested, not even water. At the end of the fast, God gave her the name of the state she was supposed to relocate to shortly. When Anita shared this news with her family, they thought she had taken the loss her senses. Nevertheless, Anita prepared to relocate. She made a final attempt to get Deacon Brown Eyes to come along with her and their son. Deacon Brown Eyes was not interested. He had started seeing one of his old girlfriends. Deacon Brown Eyes was quite comfortable living with his mother. Anita and her son relocated to another state, where they faced some of life's greatest challenges.

A note to the reader

The Bible says that we are to be anxious for nothing [Philippians 4:6]. Sometimes it seems as if God is not moving fast enough for us. Therefore, we feel the need to help him out regarding the plans he has for our lives. How sadly mistaken we are when we try to give God a hand! Our thoughts are not his thoughts, and our ways are not his ways [Isaiah 55:8-9]. Wait on God! It may seem like he is taking forever, but his timing is perfect.

CHAPTER 7

The Church

Anita relocated to a state that she, of her own volition, would never have moved there. She procrastinated regarding this move. Anita's procrastination almost cost her life. God was telling her to prepare to relocate to the state of Delaware. However, she wanted to move to Virginia. Anita kept ignoring the voice of God but instead prepared to move to where she wanted to move. She learned the hard way not to ignore the voice of God. Anita was warned by God in a dream that if she did not obey him, that she would be killed in a car accident. She ignored the dream. The next day as she was driving along a two-way street, she became very sleepy. Anita fell asleep behind the wheel of her car. Her feet automatically pressed down on the accelerator, which propelled the car faster. Anita's car crossed over into the opposing lane. She was going head on into another car. The other motorist was a female driver with two children in the back seat. The motorist in the opposing lane was blowing her horn hoping to wake

Anita up. Just before the cars collided, Anita woke up. She jerked the wheel in the direction of the lane she was supposed to be traveling in. Anita began to cry. The other female motorist was crying, and so were her children. Anita got out of her car to see if everything was all right. The other motorist was too angry and in a rage to answer her. Anita kept apologizing. However, the other motorist never responded. The other motorist just pulled off with her two children. Anita did not get a chance to give them her home phone number and vehicle information. She went home and prayed. Anita told God, "You win. I will go wherever you want me to go." She relocated to Delaware. God lead her to this awesome deliverance ministry. The pastor was a young widower with two teenage children.

The ministry was quite large. Anita asked God what she could do in a ministry of such great magnitude. The ministry appeared not to need any more help. Anita was prompt by the Holy Spirit to join the ministry. She and her son joined hoping they were not making a big mistake. It is an old saying that things seem fine in a church until you place your name on the membership roll. Anita enjoyed the way the pastor preached and taught. However, she ran into some nice nasty women. Three of them approached her at separate times. They wanted to know if she was married. Coincidentally, all three of the women claimed to be in a romantic relationship with the pastor. Anita knew off the back some of the women in the church were going to be trouble. Anita had not realized the true reason why God sent her to this ministry. However, she was about to find out. Some of these women formed a friendship with Anita. She was so desperate for friends she ignored the obvious. They were about to set her up. These women claimed to have known the pastor very well. They would pose hypothetical situations to Anita and ask her what her view on it was. Out of ignorance, she answered them overriding the still small voice, which told her not to comment on anything they said. Anita contributed the voice that told her not to speak, as being the devil. How twisted she was! These women would take poisonous input back to the pastor. They would bring back to Anita poisonous input back from the pastor. Anita had an issue that God was about to deal with very quickly. She wore her emotions on her sleeve.

Anita always sought affirmation and acceptance from those in leadership. God was about to give her a spiritual immunization for all of her issues and hang-ups. Anita was crushed when she heard what her pastor was supposed to have said allegedly. She thought how he could have said or thought those things about her. After all, he did not know her. Anita's perception of the pastor changed. It seemed that he was cold towards her. He did not appear to be friendly like before. Anita began to watch those who had come to her with their hypothetical situations. They appeared to be happier than a bug in a rug. Some of them noticed her sad continence and told her it was probably time for her to move on to another church. They also told her that God probably was trying to show her that her time was up in the ministry. These same women also stated they saw the way the pastor treated her meanly, and they did not know why he was treating her that way. They appeared to be showing genuine concern. However, they wanted her to move out of her place in God and the church. All of this deeply hurt Anita. She began missing services sporadically. Eventually, she got the nerve up to call herself leaving the ministry for good. What a mistake that was! Anita ran into all kinds of storms in her life. No matter how much and how long she fasted, God kept telling her to return to the church. Anita begged God not to make her go back. She began to tell God that he saw all the cruel things she had experienced at the church. Anita had lost her car shortly after she joined the church. She began asking some of her sisters in Christ for rides to church. When she was complaining about the things she was experiencing from nasty acting member and was planning to leave, she always had a ride to church.

However, when she began to realize that many of the people just wanted her out of the church, Anita began to shut down and kept silent. In doing this, her opportunities to receive a ride to church became less and less. There were times she stood dressed waiting for a promised ride and the person never showed up. Other times a promised ride would go out the back entrance of her housing development to avoid picking her up. Anita asked outright for a ride from a saint who attended the same church. The response was that they could not take anyone in their car. It seemed that all avenues were blocked for her to get to church. She reminded God of all of this. God still insisted that she return to the church. Not only did she have to return to the church, but also, she had to go to the pastor and apologize for her actions. Anita had to return to her place of disobedience. Anita did what God told her to do. That was the hardest thing that God had ever asked her to do. She felt embarrassed, foolish, and awkward when she returned to the church. Many were surprised to see her because she was absent from church for so long. After service, she approached her pastor to apologize. The humiliation she felt was indescribable. She had wished the ground would open and swallow her. When she approached her pastor, he listened attentively, and he prayed with her.

Then he embraced her like a father. Anita for the first time felt the love coming from her pastor like a father who cared about a child. It reminded her of the story in the Bible about the prodigal son [St. Luke 15:11-24]. When Anita arrived home that night after church, God began to deal with her. He began to tell her why she had to experience all that she had. God also told her what her purpose was in the ministry and why the devil wanted her out of the church. God began to tell her from her youth that she had always sought attention, acceptance, and affirmation from others. He told her that the enemy would use these things as a snare to hold her back in ministry. He had to inject her with feeling rejected, loneliness, and not being recognized to immune her against these things. Where he was taking her in ministry, she could not afford for any of these things to surface. If they surfaced, it would cause her to lose her focus as to what God has for her to do. As a result of this many souls would be lost. God went on to tell her, don't look to be on the scene in this ministry. She was chosen as one to be behind the scene. God reminded Anita that from her youth he had called her to a life of prayer and fasting. God told her that she was sent to cover the pastor in fasting and prayer. He pointed out that when those women approached her, she was supposed to begin to pray and fast against the spirit that was trying to permeate in the church. Not entertain it! God also told her that she was not to accept any preaching engagements for the rest of the year. He wanted her to be stable and attend her church services faithfully. God told her to sit at her leader's feet and eat all that was given out spiritually. This was a hard thing because Anita did not like being idle. However, she had to be still and allow God to complete work in her. Anita obeyed God and experienced such a freedom in the spirit. Many people's attitude did not change towards her. However, her attitude changed towards them. Anita saw her past differently. God showed her the pastor's, heart. She was wrong about so many things and began to repent all over again for even thinking the things she once thought. Anita had realized she had messed up badly. Anita had never really had a pastor-member relationship with a pastor. She did not know how! God promised her that would change. God told her that he was going to heal her in that area. He also told Anita that one day she would pastor.

God said that the same way she covered her pastor, that when it was her turn, he would send someone to cover her. Anita became content in her God given position in the church. She did not accept any preaching engagements as ordered by God. Anita sat attentively and learned everything she could from her pastor. She thanked God for her pastor and all that she was learning in the ministry. Anita thought she knew all there was to know about ministry. However, under the leadership of this young pastor, she learned about the pain and heartaches that come with the ministry. Anita remains faithful to the things of God and the ministry until God sees fit to elevate her to the next level.

A note to the reader

Realize that there is no such thing as a perfect church. However, there are churches that God had divinely appointed us to attend. Beware of those in the church who may possess the spirit of jealousy, disobedience, and insecurities. These people are a pastor's nightmare. They tend to sow discord among the brethren. These people will try to paint a bad picture of the pastor, in hopes that you will be foolish enough to leave. However, if you leave they have everything to gain, and you have everything to lose. Don't entertain foolishness! When approached with nonsense, bring it to your leader's attention and give names. This will bring an end to the madness. If they feel you are going to tell everything they said, they will not dare tell you anything. Pastors and church

members are not perfect. Don't leave because they seemingly aren't handling things the way you think God wants them to. Remember affirmation comes from God alone! Pray and fast for them. You can do more damage in the spirit realm with fasting and praying than you can with talking or having an attitude. You never know God may have sent you to a church to make a difference. Not openly, but secretly. You may be God's secret weapon with fasting and prayer! Therefore, do not be too hasty about a pastor or church. You never know maybe God has sent you to be a secret weapon in your church.

Printed in the United States
By Bookmasters